Iridessa, Lost at Sea

This edition published by Parragon in 2011
Parragon
Queen Street House
4 Queen Street
Bath BA1 1HE, UK
www.parragon.com

ISBN 978-1-4454-4074-3

Printed in China

Iridessa, Lost at Sea

Written by Lisa Papademetriou
Illustrated by Judith Holmes Clarke,
Adrienne Brown & Charles Pickens

Bath · New York · Singapore · Hong Kong · Cologne · Delhi
Melbourne · Amsterdam · Johannesburg · Auckland · Shenzhen

Iridessa snapped her fingers, and
sparks flew from her fingertips. The
sparks twinkled briefly before they
were snuffed out.

Iridessa was a light-talent fairy,
and she was practising for the Full
Moon Dance.

The next full moon was still many
nights away. Most light-talent fairies
hadn't even begun practising yet. But

Iridessa wanted to be absolutely perfect.

Iridessa spun through the air and then turned to watch the trail of sparkles fade into the darkness behind her. Three sparkles had escaped and were not in the right order. Many fairies wouldn't have noticed, but Iridessa did. She sighed. "Not quite perfect," she muttered. "Yet."

Suddenly, Iridessa heard a flutter and a low hoot. Something with large wings flapped overhead.

Iridessa dove into a nearby bush for shelter.

An owl landed next to the bush. She saw a round, yellow eye peering in at her.

Iridessa held her breath.

The owl hooted again and then pecked at the bush with its sharp, curved beak. He kept his fierce yellow eyes trained on Iridessa. She was trapped!

Suddenly, she had an idea. She snapped her fingers, sending out a streak of blinding light. The owl hopped backwards, surprised. He blinked twice, then flew away.

Iridessa stayed in the bush for several minutes. Finally, she poked her head out. There was no sign of the owl. Iridessa flew to the Home Tree as fast as she could.

"All-fairy meeting!" Iridessa shouted, as she flew down the hallway. "In the courtyard! Right away!"

Iridessa flew through each branch of the Home Tree, banging on doors and sounding the alarm. By the time she reached the courtyard, it was packed with sleepy fairies and sparrow men.

"What's going on?" someone called to her. "Why did you drag us out of bed?"

"I was just attacked by an owl!" Iridessa announced.

The fairies gasped.

Beck, an animal-talent fairy, flew

over and landed next to Iridessa.

"Fawn and I found the owl's nest not ten frog leaps from the Home Tree. It wouldn't talk to us. The owl was completely wild."

"Ten frog leaps is too close," said a sparrow man named Chirp.

"So what are we going to do?" Tink asked.

Just then, Queen Clarion flew into the courtyard. She looked around at the frightened fairies and sparrow men. "It seems we have a very serious problem," she said.

"We do, Your Majesty," Iridessa agreed.

"We must find a way to make the

owl move. What we need in this situation," the queen said, "is an organized fairy. Someone brave and clever enough to think of a way to make the owl go away."

Maybe someone like Fira, Iridessa thought. She's brave and clever. Or Rani, although she isn't very organized.

"It seems to me that *you*, Iridessa, are the perfect fairy for the job," the queen finished.

"Good idea!" Beck said. "Iridessa is the smartest, most organized fairy in Pixie Hollow!"

Iridessa was about to protest. But she looked out at the crowd of

fairies and saw their eager, hopeful
faces. Then she glanced at Queen
Clarion. The queen was smiling at
her. Iridessa swallowed hard.

"All right," Iridessa agreed. "I'll
think of something."

Iridessa stared at the birch-bark paper in front of her. She was sitting at her desk with her chin on her hand. She had barely slept all night. Instead, she had been up trying to think of ways to get the owl out of Pixie Hollow.

There was a knock at Iridessa's door, then Tinker Bell popped her head inside. "Don't mind me!" Tink said. She opened the door all the way, and the scent of freshly baked cinnamon rolls wafted into the room. "Since you didn't come to breakfast, I brought you some of Dulcie's cinnamon-pecan rolls."

She placed a tray on Iridessa's desk. The tray held a pot of tea and a plate of rolls dripping with gooey icing.

Iridessa's stomach gave a low rumble. She hadn't realized how hungry she was.

"Thanks, Tink," she said. She poured herself a cup of tea and settled back into her chair. She waited for Tink to leave, but Tink didn't go anywhere. Instead, she perched at the foot of Iridessa's bed.

"So what have you come up with to get the owl to leave?" Tink asked.

Iridessa glanced at the list in front of her. "I have sixty-eight ideas," she said. "But I don't need sixty-eight ideas. I need one good idea."

"Maybe some of the ideas are better than you think," Tink said. "Read me your best one."

Iridessa looked at her list.

"All right," she said at last. "Here's number thirty-five. 'Surround the owl. Then make loud noises with leaf whistles and walnut drums to scare it away.'"

Tink pursed her lips. "That sounds dangerous."

"I know," Iridessa agreed. She crossed number thirty-five off her list.

"What about number sixteen? 'Use smoke to drive the owl from the tree.'"

Tink shook her head. "Fire is hard to control."

Iridessa crossed that idea off her list, too. She read Tink a few more. Each one was either too dangerous, too silly, or just plain impossible.

"This isn't helping!" Iridessa crumpled the paper and tossed it into a corner of the room.

"Let me see that," Tink said. She picked the paper up and smoothed it out on Iridessa's neatly made bed.

"What about this one?" Tink said. "Number twenty-one. 'Put a light in the tree so that the owl thinks it's always daytime'. That's a great idea! Owls only hunt when it's dark. All we have to do is figure out how to make a light. That should be easy. You're a light-talent fairy, after all."

Iridessa thought for a moment. "We could ask the fireflies and glowworms to help."

"They'll probably be afraid of the owl, too," Tink said. She tugged on her bangs.

Iridessa took a bite of a cinnamon-pecan roll. "Maybe I could capture some sunbeams," she said slowly, "and put them in a bottle." Iridessa frowned. "But it would have to be a pretty big bottle."

Tink smiled brightly at Iridessa. "So let's go out and get one!" she said.

Iridessa and Tink flew to the workshop of the glass-blowing-talent fairies.

"We have lots of bottles," said Melina. She led Tink and Iridessa through the workshop.

Iridessa watched a fairy pull a long, hollow glass rod from a white-hot oven. The glass at the end of the rod was a half-melted blob of orange. Puffing her cheeks, the fairy blew on the cool end of the rod. The orange blob began to grow into a small sphere.

Melina caught Iridessa's glance. "Believe it or not, that's going to be a beautiful vase. Ah! Here we are. Bottles." Melina pointed to a shelf. "This is a big one," she said. She took down a red bottle the size of an acorn.

Tink and Iridessa exchanged a look.

"Um, do you have anything – bigger?" Tink asked.

"Bigger than this?" Melina was clearly surprised. "Well, as a matter of fact, we do. The biggest this talent has ever seen!"

She flitted over to a wooden crate and pulled off the top. Inside was a large, round, pale blue jug. "Isn't it enormous?" Melina said, taking it out.

Iridessa sighed. The bottle was about the size of a lemon – absolutely huge by fairy standards. But it wasn't nearly big enough for what she had in mind.

After thanking Melina, Tink and Iridessa flew outside.

"There has to be a way to get a bigger bottle," Tink insisted.

"They don't exist," Iridessa said.

"Sure they do!" Tink replied. "I've seen one. In Captain Hook's quarters aboard the *Jolly Roger.*"

Iridessa threw up her hands. "How in Never Land could we get a bottle from Captain Hook?" she asked.

"Well, it's not as if you have any better ideas!" Tink shot back.

"Any idea would be better than yours!" Iridessa cried. "Are we supposed to *ask* Captain Hook for a bottle? Or swipe it from under his nose?"

"Maybe I will," Tink said. Her blue eyes glinted dangerously.

"You do that." Angry tears sprang into Iridessa's eyes. I've wasted the whole morning with Tinker Bell, she thought. And I still don't have a plan! "I'm going back to my room to work on some more ideas."

"Fine," Tink snapped.

"Fine," Iridessa snapped back.

Iridessa went back to her room and halfheartedly scribbled down some new ideas. But she felt so terrible about her argument with Tink that she had trouble concentrating. Finally, she decided she should make up with her friend. After all, Tink had only been trying to help.

She ran into Beck outside the

Home Tree. "Beck, have you seen Tink?" Iridessa asked. "I need to talk to her."

"Isn't she in her workshop?" Beck said.

Iridessa shook her head. "I just checked. She wasn't there."

"That's funny." Beck perched on a toadstool. "I bumped into her a little while ago. She was in a hurry. She said she had to get something to help you with the owl problem. How's that coming, by the way?"

"Oh . . . it's fine." Iridessa's mind was racing. "Beck," she said slowly, "which way was Tink heading when you bumped into her?"

Beck thought it over. "Hmm," she said. "I was herding the baby chipmunks back towards their nest. So I guess it must have been that way."

Iridessa gasped. Beck was pointing in the direction of Pirate Cove! "Oh, no!"

"What's wrong?" Beck asked. But Iridessa was already flying away.

She knew just where Tink was headed – to the *Jolly Roger,* to get a giant bottle from Captain Hook!

The *Jolly Roger* loomed like a mountain off the coast of Never Land. Iridessa was startled by its

size.

How will I ever find Tink? she wondered.

Iridessa flew around the ship and peeked over the bow. A pirate with shaggy white hair was singing a cheery song as he mopped the deck. Another pirate with beady eyes sat nearby, coiling rope.

But Tink was nowhere in sight.

Iridessa frowned. Tink said she saw bottles in Captain Hook's quarters, she thought. Where would they be?

At that moment, a tall man in a long, scarlet jacket stepped through a door. His black curls spilt from under a wide three-cornered hat. He had a big moustache. And in the place where his left hand should be, there was a fierce-looking hook.

"Smee!" he bellowed.

"Yes, Captain?" Smee answered.

"Smee, I've finished my lunch," the captain announced. He walked up the steps to the front of the ship.

Now was her chance! Iridessa
darted through the door.

She heard a clatter as soon as
she flew into the captain's quarters.
Tinker Bell was struggling to lift a
huge bottle made of clear glass. But
it was too heavy for her. She had
only managed to knock it over.

Iridessa flew to her friend's side.
"Quick – hide!" she whispered.

"Dessa?" Tink's blue eyes widened
at the sight of her friend. Heavy
footsteps sounded outside the door.

"There's no time! Get in!" Iridessa
said. She shoved Tink towards the
bottle's open neck. Then she pulled
a napkin over the bottle and climbed

in after Tink.

They heard a cheerful humming. Smee came into the room. He collected the dishes from Captain Hook's desk and dumped them onto the tray beside the bottle. "We mustn't lose this!" Smee said as he popped the cork back into the bottle. The fairies felt the bottle being lifted up.

Smee carried Captain Hook's lunch tray down to the kitchen in the belly of the ship.

Then the humming and footsteps receded. The fairies waited for a few minutes. "It's all right," Tink said. "I think the kitchen is empty.

We're safe."

Iridessa breathed a sigh of relief. "Great," she said. "Now let's get out of here before anyone comes back!"

Tink kicked at the cork,

but it didn't budge. "It's stuck," Tink said. "I can't get it out."

"Let me try," Iridessa said. She pulled Tink aside and tried to push the cork out of the bottle. It held fast.

"It's stuck," she told Tink.

"I just said that," Tink grumbled.

Iridessa frowned. "It's your fault we're stuck here!"

"My fault?" Tink cried. Her glow turned pink.

"You're the one who had to get a bottle from Captain Hook!" Iridessa cried.

"Well, you're the one who needed a bottle!" Tink snapped.

Just then, the fairies heard footsteps again.

"Quick!" Tink said. She crouched and pressed her hands against the curved side of the bottle. "Push!"

Iridessa joined Tink and pushed. The bottle rolled forwards.

It bounced over the edge of the tray and kept rolling. "Whoa!" Iridessa cried. The napkin fell away, and she saw that they were rolling down a chute. And the chute led right out a porthole!

"Stop!" Iridessa cried. The fairies tumbled around inside the bottle as it dropped through the porthole.

Sploosh!

They landed in the water.

Right away, a wave washed over the bottle. Iridessa closed her eyes.

"It's okay, Dessa," Tink said. She patted her friend on the back. "We're safe here."

Iridessa opened her eyes. The bottle bobbed in the water. On the other side of the glass, the sea was up to their waists. But inside, they were perfectly dry.

"I wouldn't exactly say we're safe," she muttered.

"Iridessa, look," Tink said. She crouched at the bottom of the bottle. A school of pretty blue and yellow Never minnows swam by. To the right, a silvery jellyfish with trailing purple tentacles, floated peacefully.

"Shhh!" Iridessa said. She was straining to hear something out in the waves.

"Don't shush me," Tink snapped.

"Listen!" Iridessa said. "Do you hear that?"

The two fairies held perfectly still. Suddenly, Tink's face went pale. Iridessa knew that Tink had heard it, too – a steady *ticktock, ticktock.*

"What is it?" she asked Tink.

Tink slowly turned to look behind her. Iridessa followed her gaze – and found herself staring at a huge yellow eye, set in scaly green skin.

"It's the crocodile!" Tink cried.

The reptile's enormous snout opened to show rows of sharp, white teeth. The fairies watched in horror as the crocodile's jaws closed around the bottle – and them!

Iridessa could barely make out Tink's face in the darkness.

She snapped her fingers and blew gently on the spark she had created. It flickered, then grew into a bright light.

"We're *inside* the crocodile," Tink said in awe.

Iridessa looked around. The belly of the crocodile was full of

strange objects. She spotted a brass candlestick, a teddy bear, a hairbrush and a straw hat. "This crocodile will swallow anything," she remarked.

"Including that alarm clock," Tink said, pointing to the clock. It let out a steady *ticktock, ticktock.*

"So that's where the sound comes from," Iridessa said. She squeezed her eyes shut. A tiny silver tear trickled down her cheek.

Tink touched Iridessa's arm. "It's okay," she said. "We'll find a way out."

But Iridessa could tell from the look on Tink's face that she was scared too.

Suddenly, the bottle shifted and rolled forwards.

"What's happening?" Iridessa cried.

"I don't know!" Tink yelled back.

The crocodile's jaws opened. Daylight poured in, along with a flood of seawater and an old boot. A second later, the crocodile shut his mouth and it was dark again.

The boot rushed towards the fairies. It rammed against the bottle. "Hold on!" Tink yelled. The bottle spun.

"There's nothing to hold on to!" Iridessa cried. She braced her arms against the sides of the bottle as it crashed into something.

A deafening ring filled the crocodile's belly.

"It's the alarm clock!" Tink shouted. "I think we set it off!"

The croc's belly gave a sudden lurch. His mouth opened, letting daylight in again. The bottle moved towards the front of the crocodile's jaws. His mouth closed, and the bottle floated backwards.

"I think he's got the hiccups," Iridessa said.

The crocodile's belly lurched again.

"Quick, Tink!" Iridessa cried. "To the end of the bottle – I've got an idea!"

There was no time to explain. Tink and Iridessa pressed all their weight against the bottom of the bottle. The neck popped up a little bit.

On the crocodile's next hiccup, the bottle washed forwards. The bottle's neck tilted up, just enough to let it float past the croc's teeth – and right out of his mouth!

The fairies sat very still, breathing hard, as the bottle travelled away from the crocodile. Iridessa blinked in the bright daylight.

"Well," Tink said with a smile, "that was some adventure, wasn't it?"

Iridessa couldn't believe what she was hearing. "Adventure?" she shouted. "We were eaten alive by a crocodile! And we're lost out in the middle of the sea!"

"We're not that far from shore," Tink said. She pointed into the distance. They could see a stretch of white sand lined with green palms. "Something is bound to come along and help us."

Iridessa folded her arms across her chest. "*Something* – like what?"

"I have no idea," Tink said. "That's what makes it an adventure."

"The only thing that will get us out of here is a good idea. And in order to think, I need quiet. So don't talk to me. You sit on that side of the bottle, and I'll sit on this one." Iridessa plopped herself down with her back to Tinker Bell.

"What am I supposed to do?" Tink asked.

"Anything you like," Iridessa said. She put her hands over her ears.

Tink sat down too. Now the fairies were back to back.

Tink sighed. "Do you have an idea yet?"

"No," Iridessa snapped.

Tink sighed again. The two friends stayed back to back, watching the shore in the distance grow smaller

and smaller while the bottle floated
farther out to sea. . . .

The bottle had been bobbing along for hours. Night fell, and the two fairies were still inside it, out at sea.

Tink stretched out on the bottom of the bottle and fell asleep. But Iridessa lay awake for a long time. She couldn't stop thinking.

Queen Clarion asked me to come up with a way to get the owl out of Pixie Hollow, Iridessa thought miserably.

49

And instead I disappeared! Everyone probably thinks I gave up and ran away.

Iridessa sighed heavily. She had given her word that she would find a solution to the owl problem. And she had let everyone down.

At some point, Iridessa finally drifted off to sleep. When she opened her eyes, the sun was rising. All around the bottle, the water shimmered and twinkled.

Tink sat up and rubbed her eyes. "Wow," she said. "It's beautiful!"

The sun was halfway up in the sky when a white-capped wave came along. It pushed the bottle into a fast-moving current.

As they zipped along, Tink leaned on her hands and knees, looking out the front of the bottle. A school of flying fish swam next to them. They shot into the air playfully and splashed down beside the bottle.

"We're finally getting somewhere!" Tink cried gleefully.

"Yeah, but where?" Iridessa asked.

"We're going to wash up on the shore. See?" Tink said. "The beach is getting closer and – Oh, look, the fish are swimming away!" The school of fish darted suddenly to the right.

"Tink!" Iridessa shouted. "Watch out!"

Both fairies let out a cry. Their bottle was headed straight for a giant rock! Iridessa squeezed her eyes shut.

But the crash never came.

Iridessa opened one eye, then the other. She was startled to find herself face to face with a beautiful creature. The creature had long, blue hair and eyes the colour of pale violets. Iridessa looked down and saw that the creature had a fish's tail.

"A mermaid," Tink whispered.

The mermaid stared through the glass at the fairies, her head cocked to one side.

"What has the sea brought us, Numi?" asked another mermaid.

Another beautiful face peered over Numi's shoulder. This mermaid had brilliant green eyes and yellow-green hair.

"It's a mystery," Numi said. She gave the bottle a slight shake. The fairies stumbled against the glass.

Iridessa tapped on the glass. "Miss Mermaid," she said politely, "we'd be grateful if you didn't do that."

"Oola, it talks!" Numi cried.

"Let me see," Oola said. She took the bottle from her friend. "Oh!" she cried. "I know what these are – they're fairies. I used to have one."

"What did you do with it?" Numi asked.

Oola shrugged and handed the bottle back to Numi. "Nothing," she said. "It was very boring."

"Boring!" Tink squeaked indignantly.

"Hey! Hey!" Iridessa tapped on the glass. "We're not boring! If you let us out, we'll show you!"

Numi tossed her long, blue hair over one shoulder. "What can you do?" she asked.

Tink rolled her eyes. "Don't bother, Iridessa," she said. "Mermaids don't care about anyone but themselves."

But Iridessa wasn't listening. She snapped her fingers, sending up

a silver spark. Then she sent up
another, and another. Soon the bottle
was swirling with sparks.

"Oooooh," the mermaids said,
their eyes wide.

"Very pretty." Numi smiled.
"What can the other one do?" Numi
asked.

Tink stuck out her tongue. She
put her thumbs in her ears and
waggled her fingers.

"Tink!" Iridessa nudged her friend. "Stop that! Maybe they can help us!"

Numi giggled. "That one's funny! I like them both! I could put the bottle by my bed. It would make a nice lamp."

"A lamp?" Iridessa cried. "Hey, no – wait! You need to let us out of here!"

"But then you'll fly away," Numi said reasonably. "You fairies don't understand how lucky you are." Numi wagged a finger at them. "You're going to live at the bottom of the Mermaid Lagoon in a beautiful castle!"

Iridessa gasped. They would never escape from there!

"We have to do something!" Tink whispered.

Iridessa nodded. The mermaids had liked her show of sparks. Maybe they would like something else that glittered.

Beyond the rock, sunlight sent sparkles shimmering like diamonds over the water. Iridessa concentrated, drawing two sparkles together. Then three. Then four. Then three more. The sparkles joined like petals on a flower. They floated towards the rock, a water-lily of light.

Oola scooped it up. Then she

tucked the glittery flower into her hair. "Aren't I beautiful?"

Numi frowned. "Give me that," she said.

"Why?" Oola demanded.

"Because my fairy made it, that's why," Numi said.

"I won't," Oola said. "It would look silly in your hair, anyway."

"But it's mine!" Numi insisted. She reached for the glitter flower, and as she did, she dropped the bottle.

Once again, the fairies landed in the water with a splash.

The bottle was bobbing out to sea again – this time in the wrong direction. It was headed away from Never Land.

"I'm hungry," Tink moaned.

Iridessa's stomach gave a low growl.

A shy flitterfish swam close to the bottle. Iridessa touched the glass, right where the fish's nose was, and it fluttered away in a swirl of bubbles.

Iridessa rested her head against the glass. Until that moment, she hadn't realized just how thirsty she was. "We have to get out of this bottle," she said.

If they didn't get out soon, they could be in real danger.

Suddenly, the bottle tipped and swayed. Iridessa looked up and saw a huge green wall of water. The wave crashed down over the bottle.

The wave roared in their ears. Then, it washed them onto a clean stretch of white sand, dotted with bubbly green seaweed.

Iridessa looked around. "Where *are* we?" she asked. In one direction, as far as she could see, white sand met blue water. In the other direction stood a lush forest. Tall, slender trees dripped with flowery green vines. Iridessa admired their pink-gold blossoms – she had never seen such flowers!

Tink grabbed her friend's arm. "Dessa," she said, "did you see that?" She pointed to something just over Iridessa's shoulder.

Iridessa turned to look.

A long, spidery leg poked out of a hole in the sand, followed by a pretty shell. The shell was brilliant blue and looked like a stone. It was also very large.

"What is it?" Iridessa whispered back.

"I have no idea," Tink said.

The two fairies stood perfectly still. Another long, blue leg poked out, then two large pincers. Between the pincers was a small head with round black eyes. The creature was a crab.

Tink's eyes were gleaming. "He can help us! Hey!" she shouted. "Hey!" She pounded on the glass with her tiny fist.

The crab looked at the fairies with his bright eyes.

Tink tapped lightly on the glass again.

The crab scrambled towards them on his long legs and waved a pincer, almost in greeting.

"It's okay," Tink said gently. "We're your friends."

The crab edged right up to the bottle. His beady eyes stared at it. Tink moved closer to the bottle's neck, tapping all the way. "We need to get out of here," she told the crab.

All at once, as if the crab understood, he clamped the cork in his giant pincer. With a twist and a pop, the cork came free.

Fresh air blew into the bottle. It smelled of the sea and of the pink-gold flowers.

"Thank goodness!" Iridessa cried. She crawled out and plopped down on the sand.

"We're free!" Tink yelled. She followed Iridessa out of the bottle.

She dropped next to the crab and planted a kiss on top of his blue shell. The crab began to scuttle away as she turned a somersault in the air.

Iridessa laughed. The wind against her face and her wings felt so good! She darted towards the waves, dipped a toe in, and then raced back to shore before the water caught up to her.

Tink stopped her somersaults and landed on the sand in front of Iridessa. "Now all we have to do is get the bottle back to Pixie Hollow," she said.

Iridessa's smile vanished. She had forgotten that they couldn't just fly back to Pixie Hollow. They had to take the bottle with them!

"How are we going to do that?" she asked.

Tink gave her a huge grin. "I've got an idea."

Iridessa pushed the cork
back into the bottle's neck. "I can't
wait to hear this one," she muttered.

"Dessa, the answer is obvious!"
Tink said. She waved a hand at the
clear glass. "All we have to do is use
the bottle as a boat. Look how far
we've already travelled!"

Iridessa shuddered. "I'm not
getting back in that bottle," she said.

"No way."

"Not *in* it," Tink corrected. "*On* it. We'll put the bottle on its side," she explained. "Then we'll tie floats to it to keep it from spinning. We can use a stick as our mast."

"A mast?" Iridessa said. "What about a sail?"

Tink pointed to the forest behind Iridessa. The pink-gold flower vines were covered with large leaves. "There." Tink tugged on her bangs, thinking hard. "But what can we use for floats?"

Iridessa snapped her fingers, sending out a silver spark. "What about that seaweed on the shore?" she asked. "Each strand has lots of little air pockets in it."

"Iridessa, you're a genius!" Tink cried. "All right, I'll make the mast and the floats."

"What can I do?" Iridessa asked.

"Braid some rope," Tink said. "We're going to need lots."

The fairies got to work. Iridessa looked closely at the pink-gold flower vines and found that they were made of many slender tendrils. She yanked several down and started braiding them together.

Before long, she had a large pile of rope. She brought it to Tink, who was weaving a thick mat of seaweed.

Tink measured the rope. "We'll need more," she said.

"More?" Iridessa asked. But she went back to the forest to collect more vines.

By the time Iridessa returned, Tink had used the rope to tie the seaweed firmly to the bottle. She had crossed two big twigs to hold the leaf sail. Then she had used some sticky sap and a pinch of fairy dust to attach the sail to the bottle.

"It's beautiful!" Iridessa said.

Tink beamed proudly. "It looks done," Iridessa said. She held out her rope. "So what's this for?"

Tink shrugged. "I don't know

yet," she said.

Iridessa planted her hands on her hips. "I made all that rope for nothing?"

"Not for nothing," Tink told her. "I just don't know what for yet."

"All right," she said. "Let's get this boat into the water."

"I'll sit at the front," Tink said. "To navigate."

"What will I do?" Iridessa asked.

"Fly behind and steer," Tink said. "You'll have to push the boat in the right direction."

"Why do *I* get the hard job?" Iridessa demanded.

"Because *I* made the boat," Tink said.

"I made the rope!" Iridessa shot back. "We should take turns."

Tink gritted her teeth. "Fine."

"Who'll go first?" Iridessa asked. Just then, she noticed a flat, white disk near Tink's feet. "We can flip this sand dollar," she said.

One side was perfectly smooth, and the other had a star pattern. "I call star," Tink said quickly.

Iridessa flipped the sand dollar so that it tumbled down onto the sand. The sand dollar landed star-side up.

"Star!" Tink shouted, leaping into the air. "I navigate first!"

9

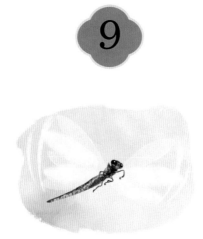

Tink and Iridessa struggled to get the bottle back into the water. Once their bottle raft was safely past the breaking waves, the wind at their backs picked up. The leaf sail puffed out as it caught the breeze.

Iridessa guided the bottle as she fluttered along behind it.

"More to the right!" Tink called from the bottle's neck.

Iridessa shoved her left shoulder against the bottle. It twisted slightly in the opposite direction.

"Perfect!" Tink cried.

Iridessa grinned.

After a while, the fairies changed places. Riding at the front of the bottle was much better.

Iridessa could see land at the horizon. Far to the left was a tiny speck of a ship – the *Jolly Roger*. If they stayed on course, they would reach Pixie Hollow.

Sooner than she would have liked, it was time to trade places again. Iridessa noticed right away that the bottle seemed heavier than before.

"What happened?" she asked.

Tink flew to the top of the sail. "The wind has died down," she said. "We'll have to push instead."

Tink flew to the back of the bottle, and the two fairies fluttered their wings like butterflies in a windstorm. They both pushed the bottle with all their strength.

Tink and Iridessa struggled along for several minutes, when Tink noticed a strange shape swimming beside them. "It's a turtle!" she cried.

Iridessa stopped and turned to look where Tink was pointing.

"He's about to pass us," Iridessa said.

"I have an idea," Tink said. She flew to the base of the mast, where she had stored the extra rope.

"What are you doing?" Iridessa called.

Tink had already tied one end of the rope around the middle of the bottle. She made a loop at the other end, then flew to the turtle. She dropped the loop over his neck.

The rope between the turtle and the bottle stretched tight. It was working! The turtle was pulling them along towards Never Land.

Tink grinned. "I told you we would need that rope."

Iridessa and Tink sat near the

front of the bottle. The shores of Never Land grew larger as they got closer. Soon they were close enough to hear the rumble of the surf.

"Tink," Iridessa said, "doesn't it look as if the *Jolly Roger* is getting bigger?"

"Oh, nuts and bolts! That's just what I was thinking," Tink admitted. "It means our friend the turtle isn't going towards Havendish Stream."

Iridessa sighed.

Tink untied the turtle.

Both fairies flew to the back of the bottle. They began pushing again. The breeze picked up a bit, and soon the bottle was sailing right towards the shore.

"I see it!" Tink shouted. "I see Havendish Stream!"

Iridessa was more tired than she had ever been in her life. But they were close now! The bottle raft bucked as they reached the breaking waves at the shore.

"We're almost there!" Iridessa shouted. She darted to the top of the sail. "Just a little to the left!"

Iridessa was about to rejoin Tink at the back, when a large wave crashed over the bottle. Instantly, Tink was soaked. She let out a choked cry as her wet wings dragged her into the sea.

"Tink!" Iridessa dove towards
her friend. She grabbed Tink's
outstretched hand and pulled her
from the water. They landed on
a beach a few feet away. Tink and
Iridessa lay back, breathing hard.

"Dessa," Tink said, "I can't fly."

Iridessa swallowed to clear the lump in her throat. How could she make it all the way to Pixie Hollow alone?

"Iridessa!" shouted a voice.

Looking up, Iridessa saw something flying toward her at top speed. She blinked.

"Beck?" Iridessa croaked.

"I've been looking for you for two days!" Beck said. "You flew off so suddenly! And then when you and Tink didn't come home last night . . ." She turned to Tink. "You're all wet!" she cried.

Iridessa explained about the bottle

and the pirates. She left out the parts about the mermaids, the turtle and the crocodile.

"So we have to get this bottle back to Pixie Hollow," Iridessa finished up.

"Maybe you two can push it," Tink said. "With a little fairy dust to make it lighter."

"Push?" Beck shook her head. "That bottle is huge. I think we'll need help." She put her fingers in her mouth and whistled. In a moment, the air was full of dragonflies.

Beck asked them to help. They landed on the bottle in a swarm of silvery wings and pulled it out of the sand. They settled it gently on Havendish Stream.

Beck and Iridessa helped Tink get on board, then climbed onto the bottle's neck. With a loud buzzing of dragonfly wings, they began speeding through the water.

Iridessa watched the scenery
streak by as the dragonflies pulled
the bottle upstream. Tink opened her
wings, drying them in the breeze.

All at once, Iridessa realized that
the banks of the stream were crowded
with fairies and sparrow men.

"There they are!" shouted a voice.
Everyone bubbled with questions as
the dragonflies slowed and brought

the bottle to a stop by the side of the stream.

"What is that thing?"

"Does it have anything to do with the owl?"

"Iridessa! We thought the owl got you!"

"Tink! Where have you been?"

"I'll explain everything," Iridessa promised. "But right now, I need your help." She pointed towards the bottle. "We're going to use this to scare the owl away." Her heart fluttered, and she added, "I hope," under her breath.

In a flash, thirty fairies darted towards the bottle. It took only a moment for them to unfasten it from the floats and mast. "We need to pull out the cork!" Iridessa cried.

Beck called a woodchuck over. With a quick yank from the woodchuck's large teeth, the cork came free.

Raising her hands, Iridessa caught a brilliant beam of light from the setting sun. She placed it inside the bottle. Then she reached for another sunbeam. Fira saw what she was doing and came to help. Then Luna joined them. Soon all the light-talents were collecting sunbeams and placing them inside the bottle as quickly as they could.

At last, the bottle was full. Beck

pushed the cork into place.

The fairies had never before seen a light as bright as this one. And it seemed even brighter a few minutes later, when the sun dipped below the horizon. Around them, the forest began to grow dark.

"We've got to get this light into the owl's tree," Iridessa said. "Before it comes back!"

Iridessa flew into the air. "This way!" she called. Behind her, dozens of fairies lifted the light-filled bottle and carried it to the owl's nesting tree.

They placed the bottle of sunbeams right beside the owl's nest. Then they bound it in place with strong spiderweb rope. The light shone in the tree as if someone had pulled the sun down to Never Land.

"Let's just hope it works," Iridessa whispered.

The fairies vanished behind leaves and into flowers that had closed up for the night. Tink and Iridessa ducked into a small knothole in a nearby tree trunk.

The owl fluttered to the tree and sat there, blinking in the bright light. It settled in its nest and tucked its head beneath its wing. But almost right away it poked it out again.

The owl hooted unhappily. It tried

to turn its back on the sunbeam bottle, but the light was still too bright. With a mighty sweep of its large wings, the owl flew off.

For a moment, the forest was silent. Then a great cheer went up. All around, the fairies came out of their hiding places.

"We did it!" Iridessa cried.

Tink beamed. "Thanks to my great idea," she said.

"What?" Iridessa frowned. She planted her hands on her hips. "Don't you mean thanks to *my* great idea?"

Tink shrugged. "You helped," she said. She gave Iridessa an

impish grin. "A little. It sure was an adventure, wasn't it?"

Iridessa shook her head. "Yes," she said at last. "It sure was."

Other titles in this series:

Beck and the
Great Berry Battle

Fawn and the Mysterious
Trickster

Lily's Pesky Plant

Silvermist and the
Ladybird Curse

The Trouble with Tink

Tink, North of Never Land

Vidia and the Fairy Crown